PAUL KROPP

D1630696

Robinswood Press

One Crazy Night
PAUL KROPP

First edition published by HIP Books 2005.
This edition published by Robinswood Press 2007.

General editor Paul Kropp.
Cover design © Robert Corrigan.
Illustrations © Andrew Gooderham.
Text design © Laura Brady.
Printed by Biddles Limited, King's Lynn.

Published by arrangement with
High Interest Publishing Inc., Toronto, Canada.

Robinswood Press
Stourbridge England
Dublin Ireland

www.robinswoodpress.com

ISBN 978-1906053-314

Todd was working alone when the storm hit. In the next three hours, he has to deal with a holdup, a woman giving birth, a clogged toilet . . . and the meanest Grade 5 teacher in the whole world.

CHAPTER 1

A Dark and Stormy Night

It was a dark and stormy night. No, scratch that opening. It's corny. To tell you the truth, it was not at all dark, and the storm didn't come until later. There was nothing at six o'clock to hint that my life would go crazy that night.

"Hey, kid," Mr. Corso barked at me. "You're on your own tonight."

Mr. Corso has to call me "kid" because he can't remember my real name, which is Todd, by the way. I've been working at his store for five months, but he still can't keep my name in his head. His store is called Corso's Italian Deli and Gas. We don't make many sandwiches, but we do sell ham, cheese and buns. We also sell gas, which explains the name.

Some people say that Corso's Deli gives you gas, but that's just a joke. No one ever buys a sandwich here, so no one would know if it gave you gas.

Corso's Deli is the only store in this town of 203 people. At least, that's the number on the highway sign now. We used to have 207 people, which made us the very biggest town on Highway 29 between Nowhere and Noplace. But then one family moved out. No one ever moves in, so I bet the numbers will keep on dropping.

"I'm on my own every night," I reminded Mr. Corso.

"Yeah, well, you're *really* on your own tonight. I'm playing poker with the guys," he said. "So don't try calling me if there's a problem. Just handle it yourself."

In five months on the job, I have never called

Mr. Corso with a problem. We never have any problems, except maybe the toilet getting plugged up. Besides, Mr. Corso has never given me his phone number.

"And don't go talking to that girl on the phone," he said — for the tenth time that week. "What's her name? Judy?"

"Julie," I corrected him.

"Judy, Julie, it's all the same," Mr. Corso went on. "You're getting paid to sell stuff, not waste time on the phone. And that includes talking to your mother."

"Yes, sir," I replied.

"That mother of yours treats you like a big baby. One of these days you got to show her you're a man. You gotta stand on your own two feet, if you know what I mean."

"You are so right, Mr. Corso."

"So don't tie up the phone here talking to your mom. I catch you on the phone one more time, you're gonna get fired," he declared. "Cell phone, store phone, any phone. You got the message?"

"Got it, sir," I told him.

Mr. Corso gave me a tough nod and then went out the door. The wind smashed the door shut behind him and I was alone.

There are not many jobs for a high school kid in a town of 203. We don't have fast food places and this is the only gas station. So if I lost this job, I'd be out of work forever — or until the end of high school. That's about the same thing.

I start work at six o'clock and close up at ten. It's four hours a night, five days a week plus a bit on Sunday. I'm supposed to be saving the money for college. My mother thinks I have to go to college to get a good job. Me, I'm not so sure. I keep telling her that I'd rather stay in town and learn a trade, but my mother doesn't want to hear that.

There is not much business on my shift. Some kids come in to rent DVDs. A few people stop their cars for gas. Some old people come in because they want somebody to talk to. A few regulars come around because they're bored. No one has ever come in for a deli sandwich. This is a good thing, because Mr. Corso has never taught me how to make a deli sandwich.

I was alone for maybe five minutes when my cell phone rang. My ring tone is the theme music to *Gilligan's Island. Ta-dum-ta-dum-ta-ta-ta-ta-dum* . . . I thought that was very cool.

I looked at the number on the screen and saw it was Julie. I've been going out with Julie for about a year, but we're having a few troubles lately. For one thing, she makes fun of my cell phone ring. Now that might seem a pretty small thing, but it's part of a pattern. Lately Julie has been making fun of my phone, my clothes, my face and my brain. But I think the real problem is that she wants more attention.

"Julie, I can't talk now," I told her. "Corso is giving me a hard time about being on the phone."

"You don't care about me," Julie replied.

"Of course I care about you," I told her. "But if Corso finds out that I'm on the phone, he'll fire me."

"Then you'll have more time to spend with me," Julie cooed.

"Julie, I gotta go. There's a customer coming. I'll . . . uh . . . I'll call you later."

That was a pretty stupid thing to say. I had just told her that I couldn't talk to her — that I'd get fired — and then I said I'd call her back. Why do I say things like that? Why don't I just act like a man and tell her that I'm working?

Because I'm afraid she's going to dump me, that's why. Not only aren't there many jobs in this town, there aren't many girls either.

I was thinking about all this when the door smashed open. It was not, however, a customer. It was my mother — carrying a bowl of soup.

"Todd, I was just passing by," she began.

"So you were just passing by with a bowl of chicken soup," I said. Any normal person would see that this made no sense, but my mother is not normal.

"And I don't want your cold to get any worse."

"I don't have a cold," I told her.

"Then why is your nose so red?"

I gave her an angry look. "Because I have a very large and embarrassing pimple coming. Because I'm a teenager and teenagers get pimples. And frankly, Mother, the red nose is bad enough with-

out you pointing it out."

My mother gave me one of her motherly smiles. "Well, dear, I'm sure the soup will be good for pimples, too."

She set down the soup on the counter in front of me. The counter was full of lottery and phone cards, but they were covered with glass. That was a good thing because my mother spilled the soup.

"Oh, my," she said, "let me just clean that up."

"It's okay, Mom," I told her. "I'll clean it later."

My mother paid no attention to me. Or maybe

she pays too much attention to me. I'm not sure which is worse. She went to the back room, got some paper towels and came back to the front.

That's when my cell phone began to ring again. *Ta-dum-ta-dum-ta-ta-ta-ta-dum* . . .

I pushed the talk button. "Julie, I can't talk to you right now — there's a customer."

"I'm not a customer," my mother shouted, "I'm your mother!"

I knew that Julie had heard that, so I tried to cover up. "Well, there's my mother and a customer. We're pretty busy here and . . . Mr. Corso gets really mad when I'm on the phone."

I don't know if there's anything worse than talking to your girlfriend in front of your mother. I mean, talking to a girlfriend is hard enough, but when your mom is listening in, it's awful.

"Yoo hoo, Julie, hello," my mother shouted.

"I got to go," I told Julie and then pushed the end button. Then I looked hard at my mother. "Mom, you've got to stop sticking your nose into my life. Mr. Corso chewed me out tonight about too many phone calls. I've got to work here, not waste my time on the phone."

"I'm not on the phone," my mother replied. "I'm right here and I brought you soup. A good son would be grateful. A good son would say, 'Thank you, Mom, for thinking about me.'"

I sighed. "Thank you, Mom, for thinking about me."

"That's a good boy," she replied. "You call me if there's any problem tonight. The weather forecast isn't good."

"Yes, Mom," I said.

"And eat your soup," she concluded. "Some chicken soup will be good for your pimple."

With that, my mother turned and went out the door. As she was leaving, she bumped into a real customer. One of the regulars but not one of my favourites.

It was old Mrs. Plotnik — the meanest Grade 5 teacher ever.

CHAPTER 2

Mean as Ever

Mrs. Plotnik used to be my Grade 5 teacher way back, like six years ago. She was old then, and she's really old now. We used to say that Mrs. Plotnik was 100 back then, so that would make her 106 right now. Anyway, you get the idea.

Mrs. Plotnik was the meanest Grade 5 teacher in our school. She might have been the meanest Grade 5 teacher in the world. She could bring the nastiest kid in town, a kid named Jimmy Branson,

to tears at least once a week. The rest of us were brought to tears once a day. Mrs. Plotnik had that kind of effect on people.

Of course, some people get mellow over time. Some old ladies become very sweet after the age of fifty or sixty. But not Mrs. Plotnik. She was mean when I was in Grade 5, and she's *real* mean now.

"Wake up, Ted, the evening is still young," she said.

"My name is Todd," I replied. People seem to have trouble with my name for some reason. In Mrs. Plotnik's case, I don't think she hears that well.

"Ted, Todd, what's the difference?" she barked. "You still having trouble with your times tables? The only boy I ever taught who didn't know his seven times tables by Grade 5."

"I'm making progress," I replied, smiling. "Now I just have trouble with my nines."

Mrs. Plotnik didn't laugh at my joke. It could be that Mrs. Plotnik didn't hear my joke or didn't get my joke. But Mrs. Plotnik didn't ever laugh. Even the day Jimmy Branson's trousers fell down, Mrs. Plotnik kept a straight face.

"What's happened to your nose, Ted?" she asked. Mrs. Plotnik was looking hard at me through the bottom part of her glasses. "It looks swollen."

"I have a cold, Mrs. Plotnik," I lied. Mr. Corso says we have to be polite to all the customers, even the crabby ones. Mr. Corso did not say we have to tell them the truth.

"Looks like a doozie of a pimple if you ask me," she replied, "but I guess it's none of my business."

Mrs. Plotnik went off to the back of the store. That's where we keep the ice cream, the rental DVDs and the ATM machine. I figured Mrs. Plotnik was looking for cash from the ATM machine. She seemed to prefer our store to the bank.

My cell phone went off just as Mrs. Plotnik got to the back of the store. *Ta-dum-ta-dum-ta-ta-ta-ta-dum* . . . .

"Why don't you get some Mozart on that thing?" snapped Mrs. Plotnik.

It was Julie, of course.

"Julie, I can't keep on talking to you like this." I delivered this in a whisper, since Mrs. Plotnik would be listening to each word. "Yes, of course I love you. But I need to keep this job, you understand. There's a customer here and I've got soup leaking into the lottery tickets. I really can't talk now."

"You hear about the big . . . ?" Julie asked me over the phone.

The sound was cutting out, so I couldn't quite hear. "What's that?" I asked her.

"You better be . . . there's a . . . ." and then all I got was silence.

I figured I'd be in big trouble now. Julie would blame me for cutting her off, so I tried to call her back right away. I had just hit "recall" on the phone when I heard a loud noise from the back of the store.

"Is everything all right?" I said, coming from behind the counter.

I found Mrs. Plotnik at the back, kicking the ATM machine.

"This stupid machine ate my card," she said, cursing and kicking. I didn't think Grade 5 teachers knew that many swear words, but Mrs. Plotnik was something else.

"Well, I'm sure . . . " I told her, trying to calm her down.

"You've never been sure about anything in your life. Now get my card back or I'll call the boss and get you fired, Ted."

"The name is Todd," I reminded her. But Mrs. Plotnik was too wound up to listen. "We just have to push the cancel button and it will pop right out."

This is true, by and large. Push "cancel" and the machine gives a little whirr and the bank card pops out. But not tonight. I pushed cancel and the machine gave a little whirr and the card stayed in. The screen was still asking for her password.

"I'm not sure what the problem is," I said. "Did you punch in your password?"

"Of course I punched it in," she snapped back. "You think I'm some kind of idiot? You young kids think that anyone my age is a fool."

"Okay, let me put in your password," I said.

"You think I'm stupid enough to give you my password?" she seemed really angry now. She had turned red in the face and, I thought, it looked like

her glasses were steaming up. "You'll clean out my account and fly to Mexico with my money, won't you?"

"Actually, I've never wanted to go to Mexico," I replied.

"You kids think all seniors are idiots."

"That's not true, Mrs. Plotnik." I did not tell Mrs. Plotnik what I was actually thinking. My actual thoughts were much worse than that.

"I want my card back and I want it now!" Mrs. Plotnik demanded. "Or I'm calling the police."

I'm not quite sure how she would call the police, since the store phone was in the back room and my cell phone was on the counter. Even if she did, it would take the police a couple of hours to show up. That's one of the problems with being halfway between Nowhere and Noplace.

Still, I could see that Mrs. Plotnik was upset. I tried to think of something I could say or do that might help. Fortunately, the front door opened as I stood there, trying to think.

It was Elaine, one of the few regular customers I really liked.

"Hi, Todd," she sang out, "and good evening to you, Mrs. Plotnik."

"What's good about it?" the old woman snapped back. "This young punk is trying to steal all my money!"

CHAPTER 3

"What Are You Staring At?"

Elaine is one of those people who is always cheerful. She has a smile on her face and a nice word for everyone — even Mrs. Plotnik. If somebody could figure out what makes Elaine so cheerful, we could sell it in pill form. *Elaine's Happy Pills*. Not only would the pills make me rich, but a lot of cranky people would be better off.

Elaine is not that much older than me, but she still looks like my kid sister. At least, she looked like

my sister until she got pregnant. Now she's eight months along . . . and counting. Elaine is as big as my uncle's cement mixer.

"This young man tried to rip off my bank card. It's bad enough this store rips me off on milk and cat food — but now it's gone too far. I'm calling the police!"

I started blushing at that. I mean, if I were two years older and Elaine were two years younger . . .

and not pregnant. Well, never mind.

"Humph!" said Mrs. Plotnik. Not many people can say *humph* any more, not even my dad or granddad. But Mrs. Plotnik had it down. *Humph!* Just like somebody from an old comic strip.

"We can't seem to get her card out of the machine," I told Elaine. "It keeps on asking for her password and won't cancel."

Elaine thought about this for a second, then came up with a great idea. "Why not just unplug the machine? It will have to reboot and spit out the card."

A stroke of genius! Maybe Elaine was really a computer geek.

I went back behind the ATM machine and pulled the plug. After a couple of seconds, I plugged it back in. The machine came back on with a grunt and a little smoke.

"Oh, dear!" Elaine said.

"Now it's *burning* my card," yelled Mrs. Plotnik. "I ask you to get the card back, and you just make things worse! You're no better than you were in

Grade 5, Ted. You're just a disaster waiting to happen!"

I pulled the plug again and the smoke died down. The store smelled a little of burnt plastic, but that was a minor problem. Mrs. Plotnik was the major problem.

"At least you can't go to Mexico on a melted bank card," sneered Mrs. Plotnik. "But how am I supposed to buy my cat food?"

"You could use a credit card," I suggested.

"And let you burn up my credit card too?" the old woman went on. "Ted, you may think I'm stupid, but I'm not *that* stupid!"

"I never said you were stupid," I replied. My voice was maybe a little loud, I admit. I was starting to lose my temper, but I had good reason. "And my name is . . . ."

I didn't get a chance to finish. Just as I was about to say "Todd," the lights went out.

I looked outside and saw that a storm had reached the edge of town. From the darkness around us, it looked as if the power was out in all the houses.

"See," said Mrs. Plotnik, proud of herself. "Playing with that bank machine has blown the fuses all over town!"

I could have tried to explain to Mrs. Plotnik that I had not — could not — blow fuses all over town. Surely someone her age knew that power sometimes went out in a storm. I mean, she had been my Grade 5 teacher! She was the woman who taught me science!

"Oh dear," Elaine said, holding on to her rather large belly. "They said a big storm would hit tonight, and now the power's gone out. I just hope my baby doesn't decide to come out in this dark."

In truth, it was not *that* dark. We still had some light from outside and the two emergency lights in the store had flipped on. If worse came to worst, I even had a couple of flashlights up front.

"I'm sure the power will be back in a couple of minutes," I replied.

KABOOM! The thunder from outside seemed to disagree.

The three of us walked up to the front door to watch the lightning outside. The thing about the

prairie is that you can see for a long way. It gives us that local joke, What's the good thing about your dog running away on the prairies?

You can watch it run . . . and run . . . and run . . . for about three days.

The good thing about a thunderstorm is that you can see an awful lot of lightning. Even before the rain hits, you can see lightning off in the distance. But when the rain hits, it can be scary.

The rain hit while we were watching. KABOOM! More thunder and the sky seemed to open up, dumping water like crazy.

As we watched, a dark figure began running toward the store. He was running fast, as if that might keep him a little bit drier. Then the front door smashed open and a wet kid came in. He looked like a real punk. I knew right away he wasn't one of our local punks but a punk from out of town.

I don't think punks look very good when they're dry. But when they get wet, they're really ugly. His spiked hair was matted down. There was water dripping off his earrings and nose ring. His leather vest and jeans were soaked.

My mother would say that he looked like something the cat dragged in. I'd say he looked worse than that.

"What you staring at?" the punk demanded.

CHAPTER 4

The Storm and the Flood

Now there were four of us inside the store. The weather outside was so bad that no one would want to leave. Even inside the store it wasn't all that nice. There was water dripping down the back wall. There was a drip right over the canned food. And there was another drip back by the washroom.

The punk went over to the DVD rack as if he were going to check one out. Meanwhile, he was

dripping all over the floor. The rest of us stood at the door, watching the storm.

"You know, Todd, this is a little scary," Elaine said. "I bet it's flooded under the Main Street Bridge. I mean, if I go into labour, how do I get to the hospital?"

"Oh, I could drive you on some back roads," I said.

"I wouldn't trust this young man to drive anywhere," snapped Mrs. Plotnik. "Not after what he did to my classroom six years ago."

"That was an accident," I said. Still, I could feel my skin turning red. Grade 5 had not been a really good year for me. The accident was just the worst part.

Our old Grade 5 classroom used to be the Kindergarten room. Maybe that's why it had a little sink in an old coat room that we used for cleaning up. One day, I was washing some paint brushes in the sink — watercolour paint, of course — when the fire alarm went off. Mrs. Plotnik told all of us to line up and get ready to leave, but I had trouble with one of the taps. I told her that I couldn't turn it off, but she didn't care. So I closed the door, lined up with the other kids and went outside.

There would have been no problem if it had been a fire *alarm*. But it wasn't. It was a fire.

Some garbage can in the boiler room had gone up in flames. Pretty soon the fire engines arrived, and we all watched the firemen go rushing in. In Grade 5, that's a real thrill. By the time they came out, it was almost three o'clock, so the principal sent us all home. I confess — I forgot all about the tap.

I didn't really see the flood. Some kids say that the water from the coat room had become a tidal wave. Other kids say that water was spurting out the windows and doors of our classroom. I don't know which is true. All I know is that there was water everywhere by the time I got to school. And I was in big trouble.

"That's a funny story," Elaine said after Mrs. Plotnik told it. "But it wasn't Todd's fault. It was just an accident."

"There are no accidents," Mrs. Plotnik mumbled. "Only idiots."

"Oh, Mrs. Plotnik, there are many accidents." Elaine smiled broadly at the old lady. "I mean, look at me. This baby is really quite an accident. Jimmy and I would never have planned for a baby right before he went off to prison." She put her hands under her large belly to make the point. "But here's our baby!" she said, grinning.

"Jimmy?" I asked, "Jimmy who?"

"Well, Jimmy Branson, of course," she replied.

"You mean Jimmy Branson is your husband?" I was close to shrieking. The idea that always-sweet

Elaine would marry the nastiest kid in town — it was too much!

"Didn't I ever tell you?" Elaine asked.

I shook my head. "No, I thought you married some guy out working on an oil field or something. How did you hook up with Jimmy Branson?" I asked, gulping.

"He just seemed so sad," Elaine replied. "His life was not going very well. He had all these problems from when he was little. I guess I felt a little sorry for him."

"A truly sad child," muttered Mrs. Plotnik. "He'd break into tears every time I talked to him."

Elaine just kept smiling, thinking of her husband. "Well, I met Jimmy when he was grown up. He seemed so kind and sweet and full of fun. He kept telling me that I was the sweetest girl he'd ever met."

Jimmy had used that same line on every girl from Grade 5 on. Of course, Jimmy was two years older than the rest of us because he'd flunked twice. He was the only 12-year-old kid still in Grade 5. No

wonder he went around beating up the rest of us.

"So we snuck off and got married," Elaine went on, "though my parents were against it. And now, well, you see what happened." Elaine gestured towards her belly.

"I repeat — no accidents, only idiots," muttered Mrs. Plotnik.

"Oh, Jimmy isn't an idiot," Elaine told us. "I'm sure when Jimmy gets out of prison he'll be a very good father." Elaine had a dreamy look on her face.

I was about to disagree when my cell phone

rang. *Ta-dum-ta-dum-ta-ta-ta-ta-dum* . . . . This time it was my mother.

"Are you . . . " she asked, her voice going blank.

"I'm fine," I shouted into the phone. "There's no power but I'm fine."

"Well . . . " There was a lot of blank air time, ". . . soup."

I pushed the end button and shook my head. Sometimes I think the world around me is just a little bit crazy, just a little off. When I think about my mother and her soup, or Elaine and Jimmy Branson, or Mrs. Plotnik . . . well, it makes me wonder. Either all of those people are crazy or it's me. Maybe they're all normal and I'm the one who's nuts.

I was thinking about that as the rain poured down outside. I might have gone on thinking about that, but the punk spoke up.

"Hey, you," he yelled, looking at me. "You work here?"

"Yeah, I'm the entire night staff," I told him. "Vice president of deli sandwiches. CEO of the pop machine."

"Pretty funny guy," the punk said. "Somebody hit your nose, or what?"

"I have a cold," I lied. "What can I do for you?"

"I want some money and some smokes," he said. He was looking at the cartons behind the counter.

"Well, the cash register won't work without power," I said. "But if you have exact change, I can sell you a package of smokes."

"Who says I'm *buying?*" the punk replied. Then he reached into his pocket and aimed something right at me. "This is a holdup!"

CHAPTER 5

Hold the Holdup

There are moments when nobody knows what to say. This was one of them. All three of us stared at the punk with open mouths.

A holdup? There hadn't been a holdup in our town since before I was born, if ever. Holdups are something that happen in big cities or on TV. The last crime I could recall was when Jimmy Branson stole a fresh apple pie from Mrs. Mappins' windowsill. That theft was the talk of the town for weeks.

It was Mrs. Plotnik who broke the silence. "A holdup? A punk like you thinks he can pull off a holdup? Where's your getaway car?"

The punk seemed stuck for a reply. "Uh . . . around the corner," he said. Then he looked down at his shoes, as if he were a bit embarrassed.

"You don't really want to do a holdup," Elaine told him. "I mean, armed robbery is a very bad thing. You could get four to ten years in prison. For what? A few cigarettes? If my husband were here, he'd tell you it's not worth it. Prison is no fun."

The punk seemed to be thinking about all this. If Elaine had been able to keep going, I think she would have talked him out of the whole thing. But then Mrs. Plotnik had to spout off.

"You're just as stupid as Ted, here," threw in Mrs. Plotnik.

"Who are you calling stupid?" snapped the Punk.

"You, child," replied Mrs. Plotnik. "If you'd taken maths from me back in Grade 5, you'd be able to figure it out. Five cartons of cigarettes for five years in prison. That's 5000 cigarettes for 1500

days out of your life. So you're saying that your life is worth roughly three smokes a day. I don't think you value yourself very highly."

The punk seemed confused by Mrs. Plotnik's maths. Back in Grade 5, I was often confused by Mrs. Plotnik's maths. Maybe that's why I had so much trouble with my seven times table back then.

"Oh, shut up," the punk replied. "You there, pimple-nose, get a box. I'm taking all the smokes you got."

Pimple-nose, I grumbled to myself, *this punk is*

not very polite. Still, he had a gun in his pocket, so I wasn't going to argue. I went off to the back room and came back with a large cardboard box.

When I got back to the front, Elaine was talking to the punk again.

"Oh, you'll regret this," she told him in her sweet, sweet voice. "Each day in prison, my Jimmy regrets what he did."

"What did Jimmy do?" I asked. I knew about his pie theft, but a kid wouldn't get prison time for that.

"He borrowed a car," she sighed.

"It must have been a pretty nice car," I said.

"Actually, it was a police car," Elaine explained. "It was kind of a silly thing to do, but he wanted to see how the siren worked. Of course, Jimmy is smarter than that now. He'll be out on parole in only a few months."

"How nice," I said. I was busy packing cigarettes into the box. I wondered if the punk was going to smoke them or sell them. He looked like a smoker, but all the different brands would be strange. He'd have to like shorts and longs and menthols.

"Faster!" the punk ordered. "Those smokes should be worth a couple of hundred bucks out on the street."

These smokes would get pretty soggy out on the street, I thought to myself. But I decided not to talk back to the punk. Isn't that what they say about a robbery — don't talk back? Still, I wondered if the punk's getaway car would start in this wet weather.

I had almost filled the box when my phone rang. *Ta-dum-ta-dum-ta-ta-ta-ta-dum* . . . .

"Ain't that the theme from *Gilligan's Island*?" the punk asked. "Pretty lame."

I decided not to get in a debate on that point. "Uh, hello," I said, flipping open the phone. This time it was my mother again.

The punk was not happy with this. He pointed the gun in his pocket right at me, then drew his finger across his neck.

I took that to mean, get off the phone — fast.

"No, I can't talk now, Mom," I told her. "We're kind of busy here at the store."

The punk drew his finger across his neck twice!

"No, everything is fine," I told her. "A couple of

leaks in the roof, but it's all just fine." Then she hit me with her big question. "No, I guess I just forgot about the soup. It's been pretty busy. I'm sorry, Mom, really. I'll heat it up . . ."

The punk drew his finger across *my* neck this time, so the choice was made for me.

"Listen, I've got to go, Mom. I'll call you later," I said, pushing the END button.

The punk held out his hand in my direction. "Better gimme the phone, guy. You're not calling nobody later."

I handed the phone over, but that's when Mrs. Plotnik kind of lost it.

"I can't stand it!" she shouted at the punk. "You make a mistake in grammar each time you open your mouth! When you say 'You're not calling nobody,' it's a double negative. Didn't you ever go to school, young man?"

The punk looked embarrassed. He turned his eyes away from my angry Grade 5 teacher and looked at Elaine. "I wasn't real good at school," he said shyly.

Elaine nodded her head in sympathy. Mrs.

Plotnik, thank the Lord, did not point out the punk's new grammar mistake.

We were all a bit surprised when my phone went off again, this time in the punk's back pocket. *Ta-dum-ta-dum-ta-ta-ta-ta-dum* . . . . He pulled the phone out, looked at it, then looked at me.

"Who's JULIE?" he asked, reading the screen.

"My girlfriend, kind of," I told him.

"Well, tell her you're real busy, 'cuz you are," the punk said.

Then he began handing the cell phone to me. I reached for it but somehow missed the hand-off. For a second, the phone seemed frozen in mid-air. Then it dropped to the floor with a crash. Little plastic bits went flying in all directions.

"My phone!" I wailed.

"No big loss," said the punk. "Get yourself a new phone with a decent ring tone."

At this point, I had good reason to be upset. The store was being robbed. I was being insulted and my cell phone was toast. My mother would never forgive me about the soup. Julie would never talk to me again. And Mr. Corso would fire me.

Things were bad . . . and then they got worse.

Outside, in the wet darkness, we saw a moving light. It was getting closer to us, heading toward the door.

"You, pimple-nose, get back behind the counter," the punk ordered. "You two women, pretend you're looking at DVDs. If you all keep quiet, nobody will get hurt."

We all took our spots and tried to look as if nothing was going on. This was not an easy thing to do, all things considered. A second later, the door crashed open. The wind blew in with one of our regular customers, a guy I called Rambo. He had a flashlight in one hand.

"Nice night," he said, flicking the water off his arms. He was a big guy, almost twice my size and built like a wrestler.

I named this guy Rambo for two reasons. First, he always dressed in army clothes. I don't know why a guy in the middle of farm country would want to dress like he was in Vietnam, but this guy did. He wasn't that old, either. I guessed he was about 25, just a little older than Elaine. Second, this

44

guy was a real law-and-order type. He'd talk to me about the way he'd fix youth crime — "send the punks to jail." When I told him about Jimmy Branson stealing the pie, Rambo thought he should have gotten ten years to life. "Teach the punk a lesson," he told me. "Cops and judges don't have any guts these days."

I was worried about what he might do to the punk. I mean, Rambo could be a pretty scary guy, but the punk had a gun. We could have bullets flying all over.

"Hi, there," I replied, trying to sound cheerful. "What could I get for you tonight?"

"Need a can of beans," he mumbled. "Can't have hot dogs without beans, can you?"

"No way," I replied.

"What's this mess on the floor?" he asked, shining his flashlight down. Rambo bent down and picked up one of the buttons from my cell phone.

"I . . . uh . . . dropped my phone," I explained.

"Must have been a cheap phone," he said.

Then Rambo saw the box half full of cigarettes. He looked at the back and saw the punk, pretending

to read a book. Then he saw Mrs. Plotnik pretending to look at DVDs.

Mrs. Plotnik never looked at DVDs. She was proud of the fact that she didn't have a DVD player. Even Rambo knew that.

"Is there something going on here?" Rambo asked me.

"Oh, no, we're all just f . . . f . . . fine." I do not stutter, as a rule, but I had a hard time getting out the word *fine*. Anyone with half a brain could see there was something wrong.

"You need some help with something?" Rambo asked.

Rambo was looking hard at the punk. He flexed his muscles, like he was ready to take out the punk with one quick punch.

"No, really, we're . . . " I never did get out the word *fine* this time, because the punk cut me off.

He spoke right to Rambo, "This is a holdup, you dork, so don't try anything funny." Then he pointed the gun in his pocket at my very large customer.

"Yaaah!" screamed Rambo. He folded his big

arms over his chest as if that might protect him. "Don't shoot me," he cried, "please, please don't shoot me!"

And then he fell to his knees.

CHAPTER 6

Let's Roll!

We had another moment when no one knew what to say. Rambo was on his knees, crying and pleading. Elaine was holding her belly, looking at Rambo with real sadness. Mrs. Plotnik stared angrily at him. Even the punk seemed to feel a bit embarrassed by all this.

Once again, it was Mrs. Plotnik who broke the silence.

"Oh, cut it out," she said to Rambo. "You're a

grown man. Stand on your own two feet."

"But . . . but," blubbered Rambo.

"Get up off your knees and act like a man," ordered Mrs. Plotnik. "If this punk is going to shoot you, make him look you in the eye first."

"Hey, really, I don't want to shoot nobody," the punk said.

"You mean, you don't want to shoot *anybody*," Mrs. Plotnik said, correcting him. "You really must work on your grammar, young man."

"Right, sorry," said the punk. "Listen, I just want the smokes and I'm out of here. I don't want to make no trouble — I mean, *any* trouble."

"Out of here . . . to where?" Elaine asked.

"I've got a cousin down in Florida," replied the punk. "He says he can get me a job at one of those big theme parks, you know, like Disneyland."

"They're not going to hire somebody like you," lectured Mrs. Plotnik. "Not unless your grammar gets better."

"Nice way to build up my self-esteem, lady," said the punk. "That kind of talk really hurts my feelings."

Now it was Mrs. Plotnik's turn to feel embarrassed.

"Sir," said Rambo to the punk. Rambo was still on his knees and looked like he was praying. "Is . . . is that your car out there under the bridge? The old Chevy?"

The punk nodded and Rambo shook his head.

"I'm sorry to have to tell you this, sir, but it's all flooded out there," Rambo explained. "Your car is pretty much under water. I don't think it's going any place."

There was a second of silence, and then the punk began swearing. He was swearing and stomping and having a tantrum — just like a two-year-old. And then, all of a sudden, he burst into tears. He was sobbing like a kid whose bike had just gotten run over by a truck.

It seemed to me that this was our big break. The punk had pulled both hands from his pockets to wipe away the tears.

So I tried to catch Rambo's eye. I figured the two of us could take down this guy. If we were quick, the punk would never know what hit him.

Rambo finally looked at me. I sent him a big mental thought — *Take down the punk!* Rambo blinked and seemed to get it, so there was no time to waste.

"Let's roll!" I cried, rushing at the punk from one side.

I thought that Rambo would rush from the other side, but no such luck. Rambo just stood there, his arms over his chest. The guy had 250 pounds of muscle, but he wasn't going to use any of it.

Fortunately, I hit the punk with a lot of force. He went sailing into the DVD rack, and soon we were both on the floor, covered with DVDs.

I kept trying to grab both of the punk's hands to keep him from getting out his gun. The trouble was, the punk kept on wiggling away. I managed to get one arm and hold it, but his other arm was still free.

"Help!" I cried.

Rambo just stayed on his knees, watching us. He seemed frozen to the spot.

But Mrs. Plotnik jumped down to help. She fell

with both knees on the punk's stomach — "oof!" — then grabbed the punk's other arm.

Now we had him! I had one arm, Mrs. Plotnik had the other and the punk was flat on his back.

"Elaine, get the gun!" shouted Mrs. Plotnik.

It was hard for Elaine to bend over to reach the punk. She had to kneel down on one side, then reach into the punk's vest pocket.

She pulled out a roll of Lifesavers.

"Not the Lifesavers, Elaine, get the gun!"

Elaine kept searching that pocket, then the other pocket and finally threw up her hands. "He doesn't have a gun," she cried.

The three of us looked down at the punk, who seemed to be in a lot of pain from Mrs. Plotnik's weight on his stomach.

"I never said I had a gun," he cried. "I just wanted the smokes 'cause I'm out of money."

None of us knew what to say. Rambo got up off his knees and I let go of the punk's arm.

"Well, you could have just *asked* for help," said Elaine. "Mrs. Plotnik and I would have given you some money."

"Speak for yourself, Elaine," snapped Mrs. Plotnik. She got off the punk's stomach and kicked a couple of DVDs under the freezer.

The punk sat up and tried to get his breath back.

"You guys hurt me," he whined. "I should call the cops and file charges against all of you."

"Except you broke my cell phone," I reminded him. "And you threatened all of us."

"Yeah, but I was real desperate. I haven't had anything to eat in the last two days. I've got maybe ten bucks to buy gas to get from here to Florida. I mean, things were bad . . . and now my car is flooded." He stopped to wipe a tear away from one eye.

I think we all felt a little sorry for the young punk. He didn't look too nice, or too friendly, or too smart. But he was a human being. He was trying to do something with his life but got a little confused along the way. Maybe it was time for us to show a little understanding.

"What's your name?" I asked him.

"Peter," replied the punk, "Peter Robichaud. My

family is up in Moose Factory, but we don't get on too good."

"You don't get on too *well*," Mrs. Plotnik corrected.

The punk looked upset. "Well, they don't like me much and were pretty happy when I left. I think maybe it was my hairstyle. They had some kind of big problem with my hair."

"You really thought you could get to Florida on ten dollars?" asked Elaine.

"Well, if I could sell this big carton of smokes . . . maybe." The punk looked around at all of us. From the look on his face, I knew his problem was more than just bad grammar. He was just plain dumb.

"I just wanted to make a fresh start," he said. "Things weren't going too good up north, and I saw this ad for Disney World on TV. They call it the Magic Kingdom, you know. So I thought maybe I'd get a little magic along the way, but it don't look like that right now."

I shook my head and started feeling sorry for the guy. "Listen," I said, "you've got to leave the smokes or else I'll get fired by my boss. But I'll just give you ten bucks for your trip. Mrs. Plotnick, what about you?"

Mrs. Plotnik didn't look too friendly, but I guess she got the message. "Well, I guess I could find ten dollars to help out. I could give him twenty if your stupid ATM machine worked."

"Elaine," I asked. "Elaine?"

Elaine said nothing. She was still kneeling on the floor, beside the punk, and holding her belly.

"Elaine, are you all right?" asked Mrs. Plotnik.

Elaine looked around at all of us, a strange look in her eyes.

"I . . . um . . . oooh . . . I . . . I'm going into labour!"

CHAPTER 7

Baby Todd

Our situation was not good. The lights were out. The only car — the punk's — was flooded. The storm was still raging outside. The nearest hospital was an hour away, even if we had a car. And Elaine was going to give birth, like soon.

"Okay, so what do we do?" I asked the others.

"I could go run and see if somebody has a car," Rambo said.

"What good would that do?" replied Mrs.

Plotnik. "Her water has broken and she's already in labour. This baby could be out in ten minutes. Better for Elaine to give birth here than on the highway."

"I'll phone 9-1-1 and get somebody to help," I suggested.

I realized that my cell phone was smashed, so I ran to the back room and picked up the store phone. The line was dead. The storm must have knocked down the phone lines along with the power lines.

"I saw this movie where a lady gives birth in a taxi," said the punk. "Like, it ain't that hard."

"Spoken like a stupid man," grumbled Mrs. Plotnik. "You try having a baby some time and tell me how easy it is!"

That's when Mrs. Plotnik took over. Maybe it was all those years of telling little Grade 5 kids what to do. She knew how to take charge.

We cleared off a flat ice cream freezer, then covered it with magazines and a blanket from out back. We had our delivery table. Rambo and I lifted up Elaine and placed her on the freezer.

I went back and started running hot water. I wasn't quite sure what to do with the hot water, but in old movies they always have rags and hot water. The punk came back to help me. He found an old sheet and began ripping it into rags.

Out in front, Elaine was groaning and grunting. Rambo held her hand. Mrs. Plotnik was kneeling down with the flashlight, looking for signs of the baby. The punk and I just stood there, waiting.

"Okay, boys, it's almost show time," Mrs. Plotnik announced. "I want each of you to hold one leg. Whatever you do, don't let go. Elaine, you've got to start pushing."

"Eyuunnnnh!" Elaine replied. We took that to be a yes.

"Have you ever done this kind of thing before?" I asked Mrs. Plotnik.

Mrs. Plotnik looked up at me. "Only in my nightmares," she replied. "I had my children in the hospital, like any sensible person. Push, Elaine."

"Eyuunnnnh!"

"This is like another movie I saw once — was it *Alien*?" said the punk.

"I hope not," I replied.

Elaine gave another groan.

"We're close," announced Mrs. Plotnik. "I can see the baby's head beginning to come out. Ted, you be ready with a blanket when I hand you the baby."

"It's Todd," I reminded her.

"Whatever," she snapped back. "And you, Peter, give me the scissors when I ask for them. We'll have to let nature handle the rest."

We would have looked pretty strange to anyone looking through the front window. Elaine was pink in the face, crying from pain and pushing like crazy. Rambo was standing beside her, holding her back up. He looked like an awkward husband in the waiting room of a hospital. The punk and I were just human clamps, trying to make room for the baby to come out. Neither of us knew what to do, so we were glad that Mrs. Plotnik was in charge.

"Eyuunnnnh!" cried Elaine, then "Eyuunnnnh!" and "Eyuunnnnh!"

"The baby's coming," said Mrs. Plotnik. "The top of his head looks just like little Jimmy

Branson's."

Then Elaine gave a loud, high-pitched cry, "Eyuunnnnnnnnh!" . . . and the baby popped into Mrs. Plotnik's hands.

"Well, it looks like we have a little boy," said Mrs. Plotnik. "It's a healthy little boy."

She pulled out a blood-covered baby that was all wrinkled and blotchy — and handed it to me.

"Ayyunh!" called Rambo when he saw the child. His eyelids blinked, he staggered and his knees buckled. Then all 250 pounds of Rambo fell to the floor.

Maybe Rambo's fall started the baby crying, or maybe it was looking up at my face. Whatever, I didn't have to spank the baby's bum. All by himself, the kid began to wail.

I couldn't blame him. The poor guy had come out from a nice, warm mother and into a cold, cruel world . . . where the first face he saw was mine. He must have said to himself, *I'm going to grow up with a face like that*, and then burst into tears. I mean, that's what I would have done.

Mrs. Plotnik was busy tying a knot in the cord,

then cutting it off. I wanted to give the baby back to her, or to the punk . . . but nobody was offering.

When Mrs. Plotnik had finished cleaning up, she turned to me. "Okay, give the baby to his mom and you, Peter, get a camera."

"A camera?" asked the punk.

"This is a store, isn't it?" she snapped back at him. "Grab one of those cheap cameras and take a picture. This is a big moment when the mother first holds her baby."

The punk went off to get a camera from the front. I stepped over Rambo and got ready for the Kodak moment. When the punk had the camera ready, I took the baby and handed him to Elaine.

"Here's your little guy," I said to the beaming mother. "Our town's population is now up by one, to 204."

Peter snapped a photo. The flash went off and the baby started crying again. Then Peter took a second photo with Elaine and the baby cuddling. At last Elaine put the baby to her breast, and Peter took one more photo.

"Pretty sweet," said the punk. "When I get to

Florida, maybe I can be one of those photo guys."

Elaine looked up at us with tearful eyes. "Mrs. Plotnik, Todd, Peter . . . I don't know what to say. You were all so wonderful. You saved me and my baby."

"Don't be silly," said Mrs. Plotnik. "Women have been having babies for millions of years, often all by themselves. We just gave you a little help."

"Well, thank you," Elaine said. "And I want to tell you all, I've come up with the name for my little guy. I'm giving him a name that might help him grow up to be a big, strong, wonderful man." She paused for a second and looked at me. "I'm going to name him Todd."

Everyone looked at me. I think the baby might have looked at me, too, but he was too busy nursing. Poor kid, going to grow up with a name that nobody gets right.

Maybe I should have given a speech right then. Maybe I should have told Elaine that I was honoured, and would work hard to be a role model. Maybe I could have said a few words of wisdom that we would all have remembered for years and years.

But just then the door blew open and we all turned to look. There, in the doorway, was a large man dressed all in yellow.

"You got a washroom here?" asked the man.

CHAPTER 8

The Power and the Glory

The store was pretty dark. We only had the emergency lights and Rambo's flashlight. So when the man came to the door, maybe he couldn't see much. But you'd think he would notice a pile of rags on the floor. You'd think he would have seen the overturned DVD rack. You'd think he would have seen a woman lying on an ice cream freezer nursing a baby.

But the guy didn't give a thought to all that.

"I gotta go, like bad!" he said.

From the way he was holding himself — kind of twisted up — I knew he wasn't kidding. We don't usually let customers use the washroom at the back, but this guy had a big problem. After all we had been through, how could I say no?

"It's at the back. The light switch is on the . . . " and then I stopped myself. There were no lights, but maybe that would change. As the man walked back, I saw big letters on the back of his yellow rain gear: HYDRO.

"Hey, I think help has arrived," I said to the others.

I wasn't sure how much help we needed at this point. The punk was busy beaming at baby Todd. Elaine was nursing her new child. Rambo was climbing from the floor. Mrs. Plotnik was helping Rambo get steady on his feet. Compared with the problems we'd been through, this was nothing.

Until the Hydro guy came out of the washroom.

"Hey, kid," he said, "you got a little problem back there. The toilet . . . you know?" He made a sign for rising water, and I knew just what he meant.

"Bring the flashlight," I told him "We've got to move fast."

As you might guess, I have this problem with water and floods. So when we started having toilet troubles at my house, I learned a few things. I learned to use a plunger so fast and so smooth that I could unclog anything. I like to think that I'm like Tiger Woods with a plunger.

I also knew how to stop the water before the mess went over the top of the bowl. But that meant working really fast with a wrench.

When I got back to the washroom, the smell was enough to knock me over.

"Sorry," the guy said, looking at my face. "Must have been something I ate."

"Turn the big valve to the right," I told him, pointing over to the wall. Then I started working with the plunger. I won't go into all the details on this since it was pretty disgusting. But I can report that we stopped a truly awful flood.

"You know, kid, you're really quite good with a plunger," said the guy.

"Like Tiger Woods with a five iron," I said.

"Uh, I guess," the guy replied. From the look on his face, I guess he wasn't into golf. "Looks like I owe you a favour or two."

I decided to pick up on the offer. "Can you do anything about the power?" I asked him. "We've got a lady who just gave birth and a guy who's pretty dizzy on his feet. A little light would sure help things."

"Yeah, sure," the guy said. "Lots of lines went down in this storm, but I can try to find where yours is broken — and I've got the truck."

"Like a big hydro truck with one of those thingamjiggies?"

"Yeah, it's called a cherry picker. Give me a minute and I'll have your power on. Then I can drive the new mom up to the hospital. I mean, your washroom was here when I needed it, so let me pay you back."

The hydro guy went off to fix our power and I went to tell the others the good news. By then, Elaine was sitting up on the ice cream freezer and the others had gathered around to admire the baby.

Baby Todd looked much better now that the

guck had been cleaned off him. He was a cute, pink little thing with tiny eyes and just a bit of dark hair.

"He's so cute," the punk said. "When he gets big, you got to come visit me in Florida."

"He is pretty good-looking for a newborn," said Mrs. Plotnik. "Doesn't look at all like Jimmy Branson except for the top of his head."

"You don't think he looks like Jimmy?" Elaine asked us.

I looked at the baby and then I looked at Elaine. "I'll give you the good news," I said, "he doesn't look *at all* like Jimmy. He looks like you, Elaine. If he's lucky, he'll keep on looking like you as he grows up."

"Ted's had some sort of problem with Jimmy ever since Grade 5," Mrs. Plotnik explained. "It goes back to that day in the playground when I had to get Jimmy's foot off your head. You remember that?"

I sighed.

I had spent years trying to forget that day. It all started when I brought this autographed baseball to school to show the other kids. Jimmy Branson said that it was his and I said no way. And that led to an argument.

Jimmy was always a bit bigger than me, and a lot meaner, so he grabbed the baseball. And then he knocked me in the stomach. I fell down and Jimmy put his big foot on my head. I struggled to get up, but Jimmy had a really heavy foot so I was getting nowhere. That's when Mrs. Plotnik came to my rescue. She took Jimmy by the ear lobe and dragged him to the office. I got my baseball back and Jimmy got sent home. And on his way home, he stole the pie from Mrs. Mappins. That began Jimmy's life of crime. And the rest, as they say, is history.

Before I had a chance to explain any of this, the lights in the store went on. The ice cream freezer hummed to life. The cash register made happy chirping sounds. At the back of the store, the ATM grunted and began to beep.

I walked back to check out the ATM and then had to smile.

"Mrs. Plotnik," I said, "I've got your bank card."

"Well, thank you, Ted," she replied. "You really are a hero today."

"It's Todd, Mrs. Plotnik," I reminded her for the umpteenth time.

The hydro guy stuck his head in the door.

"Somebody here need a ride to the hospital?" he asked.

Elaine looked at the baby, then up at all the rest of us. "No," she said sweetly, "I think we're just fine."

"Okay, I've got some lines to fix. Nice to meet you all," he said and then went off with a wave.

The rest of us enjoyed the light and the end of the storm. I was about to start making everyone ham and cheese sandwiches when the door opened one more time.

There in the doorway was Mr. Corso, my boss. He took one look around the store and his face quickly turned from a smile to a frown.

"What's this awful mess? What's going on in my store?"

CHAPTER 9

Mr. Corso Is Not Amused

I suppose the store did not look very good at that moment. There were pieces of cell phone on the floor. DVDs had gone flying everywhere. And there was a pile of messy rags by the back wall. Still, considering what we had been through, it wasn't that bad.

"You, kid, what you do?" demanded Mr. Corso. "What kinda mess did you make of my store?"

Mr. Corso was a short man with a tall temper.

He kept stomping around the store as if he owned it. Well, actually, he did own it, but he was giving us all a lot of attitude.

"We had quite a night," I told him. "I mean you wouldn't believe what happened."

Mr. Corso was not amused. "I go out one night to a poker game — one night — and I come back and my store is busted. What'd you do? You open the door so the storm blows right through here. And what's dat smell? It's like there's a dead guy in the back room."

"Well, you see, the power went off and the plumbing backed up —"

Mr. Corso cut me off. He walked right up and looked me in the eye. This was not easy, because Mr. Corso is so much shorter than I am. He must have been standing on his toes.

"I was gonna fire you because of the phone," he said. "But now I'm gonna fire you because you made a big mess. Kid, you are done, finished, kaput!" He was on a roll now. "I don't ever want to see you in this store again, not ever, not for nothing!"

I didn't know what to say, but Mrs. Plotnik came to my rescue. "Corso, stop acting like an idiot," she said. "You better thank your lucky stars that Ted here — I mean, Todd — has such a level head. We've had a storm, a power failure, a baby being born and a flooded washroom. You come in to find a little mess — so what? At least you still have a store."

"All this happened tonight?" Mr. Corso asked.

"That's right," Mrs. Plotnik went on. "And Todd was able to handle all of it. He helped us deliver this baby and, if you ask me, he was a hero tonight."

"The baby was born . . . here?"

"In the middle of the storm, on the ice cream freezer, with no power," Elaine explained. "We couldn't have done it without Todd and Peter. I'm sorry about the mess, Mr. Corso, but there was no way to get to the hospital."

Mr. Corso went over and looked down at the now-sleeping baby. He ran his thick fingers over the baby's hair. "Pretty cute *bambino*."

Elaine smiled at his words. "I've named him after Todd, because of tonight."

Now I was blushing.

Mrs. Plotnik added to the praise. "Not only that, Todd got my bank card back from your stupid machine. Corso, if you fire this boy, I'll tell everyone I know to stay away from your store. If you were smart, you would give this young man a raise."

"A raise!" Corso cried. "He can't even make a ham and cheese sandwich, this boy."

"But he keeps his cool in times of stress," said Mrs. Plotnik. She turned to me with a smile. "It all goes back to those lessons I taught him in Grade 5. He wasn't good in maths, mind you, but he does have other talents."

"Really?" Mr. Corso asked.

"Really," Mrs. Plotnik replied. "You had better start treating Todd a little better after all this. He's grown up to be a fine young man and you should be proud that he's willing to work for you."

"Proud of this kid?" he asked, looking at me.

I figured it was my turn to speak up. "That's right, Mr. Corso. If you'd have been here, you would have been proud of me," I told him. Because at that moment, I was very, very proud of myself.

CHAPTER 10

No More Chicken Soup

I think we all decided to forget about Peter's attempt at "robbery." The guy had enough problems without all that. He had been desperate, really, and there was no gun. Besides, he really was a big help with Elaine and the baby. Maybe his grammar was bad, but he was a pretty nice guy deep down.

After the storm, Rambo went to help Peter get the water out of his car. It was a couple of days before the car dried out. Rambo let Peter stay at his house until he could get going. The two of them seemed to get on pretty well, and Rambo says he's going to visit him down in Florida.

At the church, we took up a little collection to help Peter on his trip. With the two hundred dollars we collected, he could travel in style. The other day, we got an email from him. He actually got a job at a theme park — one of those guys who walks around in a big animal suit. He thinks it's the best job in the world. "I make little kids happy, all day long. What could be better?"

Rambo has mellowed out a little. He's dropped his "tough guy" pose because we all know better. Elaine made him godfather to the baby, and he likes that role. It gives him an excuse to drop by and watch little Todd grow up. It also gives him an excuse to see Elaine.

Jimmy Branson, you see, never came back to our town. When his parole came up, he went to a halfway house in Winnipeg. Then he disappeared. I guess Jimmy Branson isn't going to be much of a dad.

Elaine still isn't over that yet. It's tough for a young mom to get dumped by her husband. But her parents are really nice and help her out a lot. And Rambo is spending a lot of time over there, not just to see the baby.

As for me, I'm still working at Corso's Italian Deli and Gas. I got a raise of ten cents an hour, but that didn't matter much. I've gotten to like the job. I like the regulars who come by. I like the ham and cheese sandwiches I've learned to make. I'm not going to do this for the rest of my life, but it's good for now.

For the rest of my life, I've got a couple of ideas. The hydro guy got in touch with this plumber here in town. He's going to take me on when I get out of high school. He says that he's never seen anybody as good with a plunger as I am.

This led to a fight with my mother, of course. She got very angry when I told her I didn't want to go to college. She won't even make me chicken soup any more. But Mr. Corso said it was a good thing to stand up to her. "Otherwise, kid, she'll run your whole life."

Mrs. Plotnik has gotten a bit nicer than she used to be. Just the other day, she was back in the store. "Just need a little cat food," she told me as she piled ten cans up on the counter.

My new cell phone rang while I saw her counting the cans. It now plays the theme from Mozart's Jupiter Symphony.

"Excuse me, Mrs. Plotnik," I said. I saw that it was a call from Julie. Now that I was a hero, she decided I could still be her boyfriend. "I can't talk now," I told her, "but I'll call you back." There were the usual complaints. "Yes, of course I want to talk to you, but I've got a customer here." I pushed the off button.

"You ever think about getting a new girlfriend, Todd?" asked Mrs. Plotnik. She gets my name right these days, at least most of the time. "Maybe a girl who doesn't call you at work so much."

"Well, I suppose," I sighed.

"I remember Julie from your class," Mrs. Plotnik went on. "You were bad at maths, Todd, but Julie was terrible. She had trouble with her five times table."

"Still does," I replied.

"You deserve somebody better, Todd," Mrs. Plotnik concluded. "After all, for at least one night you were a hero."

Some of the other titles in this series:

Against All Odds
PAUL KROPP

Nothing ever came easy for Jeff. He had a tough time at school and hung around with all the wrong kids in the neighbourhood. But when he and his brother are drowning in a storm sewer, Jeff is the one who never gives up.

Hitting the Road
PAUL KROPP

The road isn't nice to kids who run away. Matt knew there would be trouble even before he took off with his friend Cody. Along the way, there would be fighting, fear, hunger and a jump from a speeding train. Was it all worth it?

The Kid is Lost
PAUL KROPP

It's a babysitter's worst nightmare: a child goes missing! Kurt has to get help and lead the search into a deadly swamp on his ATV. Will he find the lost child in time?

Caught in the Blizzard
PAUL KROPP

Sam and Connor were enemies from the start. Sam was an Innu, close to the Arctic land that he loved. Connor was a white kid, only out for a few thrills. When a blizzard strikes, the two of them must struggle to survive in the frozen north.

The Bully
LIZ BROWN

Sugar and spice and everything . . . mean. Allison finds that the worst bully at her school is a girl, and the worst weapon can be a whisper.

Hacker
ALEX KROPP

Computer crime hits a high school, and the prime suspect is a teacher. Hacker and Cole have to find who's behind the mess before the football team breaks them in two.

Avalanche
PAUL KROPP

It was just a school trip, just a winter hike through the mountains. But when a wall of snow comes sliding down, fifteen kids have to fight for their lives. Not all of them will win the fight.

Running for Dave
LORI JAMISON

Rusty always felt second-best. He wasn't a winner on the track team or in the eyes of his parents. But when his best friend gets cancer, Rusty is given a challenge he just has to meet.

About the Author

Paul Kropp is the author of many popular novels for young people. His work includes six award-winning young adult novels and many 'High Interest' novels, as well as writing for adults and younger children. His books for young adults – *Moonkid and Prometheus* and *Moonkid and Liberty* – have been translated into many languages, including German, Danish, French, Portuguese and Spanish, and won awards across the globe.

With the publication of revised editions of his High Interest novels by Robinswood Press, Paul Kropp's expertise in providing exciting reading, with the reading level carefully controlled, is now extended to a wider audience of English-speakers in the UK, Ireland and beyond.

Paul was born in the 1940's in Buffalo and studied at Columbia University in New York and later at the University of Western Ontario. Having taught for many years in Canada, he now lives in an 1889 town-house in Toronto's Cabbagetown district with his wife, Lori Jamison. Both Paul and Lori are popular speakers and lecturers, for teachers and librarians worldwide, on issues related to reading.

For more information on the High Interest series
and other Robinswood titles, visit
www.robinswoodpress.com